# Parachute Man

## by

## Christopher Ball (aged 10)

## Illustrated by Anne Tilby

Grosvenor House
Publishing Limited

This book is published by
Grosvenor House Publishing Ltd
Link House
140 The Broadway, Tolworth, Surrey, KT6 7HT.
www.grosvenorhousepublishing.co.uk

This book is a work of fiction. Any resemblance to
people or events, past or present, is purely coincidental.

A CIP record for this book
is available from the British Library

ISBN 978-1-83975-736-5

# Parachute Man

For all the boys and girls who've played
and made stories with us

Last Thursday Miss Fell said we had a special visitor. We wrote our names on sticky labels as usual.

A tall man came into the hall with a hat and a big bag, which didn't look that special but anyway...

He said, "There's water deep inside my bag. Please help me pour it out."

I felt sorry for him because he was weird but Miss Fell was looking at me. So I listened.

"Give me some words that describe watery sounds."

Right. Well, we have these 'wow' words on our classroom wall that Miss tells us to use, which we usually forget. We guessed he wanted them so straightaway we shouted…

Gurgling           spurtling

rushing           whooshing

flooding     ROARING!!

Miss Fell stared at us and then at him.
We went quiet.

The man said,
"Let's make a circle and sit."

Miss Fell sort of nodded at him, as he said,
"We will share a wonderful story soon but first we need a
world with water for our tale.

Water will only flow quietly drip by drip.

Could someone with careful hands open up my bag and
gently release the water?"

My friend Rachel, who is nine and kind, reached into his bag and, with a finger and thumb, slowly drew out a soft piece of cloth which, I suppose, did look a bit trickly as it fell.

The man helped her pull the material and spread it out like a big, round pool. The funny thing was, there were lumpy parts which took ages to sink.

I watched till they were flat.

Well, the cloth was flat in the end, when James stopped fiddling with it.

"And **finally** – thank you, **James** – let's make our
water freeze…..like ice,"
he said, drawing it tighter.

"This huge circle is silk. It was a parachute but now it's
magic and is whatever we want.
(Definitely over the top in my opinion)
Listen," The man said.
"Hold the edges, everyone. Together. Lift. "

We picked it up and felt the wind as it rose like
waves swaying from side to side.

"Let's say things that remind us of the sea," he said.

Michael said, "Ripples."
Terry said, "Rolling waves."
Gill said, "Giant billows."
Araminta said, "Spuming Surf."
(I'm not sure what that meant but she wrote it in my book later.)
Rachel said, "Seahorses."

Every time someone spoke, he demonstrated how to make the parachute come alive like their words.

The ripples turned into rolling waves, the rolling surfed against the sand and the seahorses **"LET GO NOW AND**

waves grew giant billows, the giant billows
galloped until Parachute Man said,
STAND STILL!"

The seahorses stood, the surf sank, the billows blew, the waves rolled, the ripples folded and the sea was smooth. James just watched this time, which might not have been magic but it was definitely a miracle.

We sat down.

Parachute Man said to hold the silky edges and pull tight.
"Let's make ice."
We heaved harder.
"It's getting… warmer…"

We shook our ice with little shivery moves until it cracked and melted and the water bubbled and simmered and boiled.

"STAND NOW!" He shouted suddenly.

The parachute rose and steamy
clouds floated upwards.

"AND LET GO NOW!"

The clouds hit the ceiling, stuck there for ages,
then fell very softly with a swishy sound.
We couldn't help running after the
parachute and laughing.
Even Miss Fell smiled a bit
when James shouted,
"MORE!"
Parachute Man said,
"More clouds?"
Everyone shouted,
"YES!"

We created wispy, woolly, windy and wild clouds and
with the parachute made them hover -  better than
'wow' words but don't tell Miss!

Parachute Man whispered,
"Clouds hang over the mountains' heads but these
mountains will be still and not run around the hall
like mad things."

We made one giant mushroom canopy and released it.
It glided skywards like an enormous bubble and fell
over our heads, drifting down.

We giggled but nobody moved.

Parachute Man said,
"Now our story...
Thousands of years ago in Greece lived the cleverest
inventor called Daedalus. He was imprisoned atop a
tall tower with his son, Icarus, by King Minos of Crete.
Minos wanted Daedalus' inventions for himself.
However, crafty Daedalus planned to escape by
making wings from birds' feathers, wax and twigs.
I will pretend to be Daedalus. Who will be Icarus?"

He picked James because, if he hadn't, James would
probably have exploded.

He put two feathers between
James's fingers, one in each hand.

James kept dropping them and
Parachute Man eyeballed
James saying,

"Icarus, my son,
do you wish to fly?"

James nodded.

"Then listen.
Do **<u>not</u>** let the feathers fall!"

Parachute Man said,
"Hold the parachute again! Haul hard."

We did. It was flat, about three feet off the ground.
Perfect for diving, thought James. So he dived.

Daedalus shouted, "**STOP**!" James froze.

"Soar slowly, Icarus! If you fly too high,
the sun will melt your wings."

James clambered into the middle and
rolled over the wispy, woolly, windy,
wild clouds of our sky.
His feathers stretched out while
we tugged tight, keeping him in the air.
He loved 'flying', so we yanked forcefully
to support his weight.
Suddenly he spun
in slow motion, which was really clever.

We chanted falling phrases…

…dizzy…panicking…**whirling**…

screaming…fading…

fearful…

headlong……

Amazingly, James acted those feelings like he **really** felt them……

29

But eventually our words were exhausted and
the silk sank. It was just like he'd hit water.

As we released the parachute, seahorses jumped and surf splashed until billows and waves and ripples covered our Icarus.

He lay there still as stone with only his hand showing.

As the last breath of air escaped from the parachute, Icarus pulled his fingers under and all that remained was a floating feather….and a wrinkle.

We stopped dead for ages.
Then Rachel pulled back a fold
of silk just to make sure that
James was OK.

And he was.

Suddenly Parachute Man
scooped up our silky sea.

"Be seeing you,"
he announced
and was gone….

P.S:
When I think about it, I'm not sure
that it was a magic parachute but it
was still pretty good anyway.

## Chris Ball

Chris Ball works in nurseries, schools and universities. He has written and co-written books, plays and teacher resources for schools, museums and theatres.

Parachute Man is based on some of his Drama workshops.


## Anne Tilby

Anne Tilby's work as an artist and designer has included creating sets and costumes for film, tv and opera. She runs art workshops for all age groups at places like the Science Museum, schools and at the odd festival or art gallery.

Lightning Source UK Ltd.
Milton Keynes UK
UKHW020837161121
394011UK00005B/337